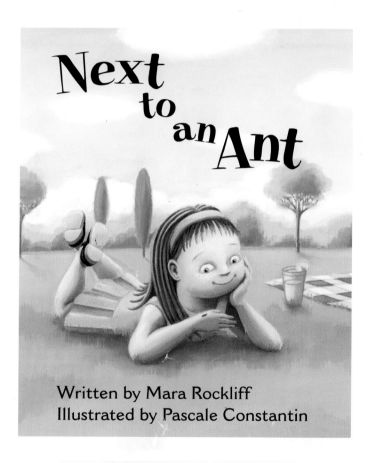

# Next to an Ant

Written by Mara Rockliff
Illustrated by Pascale Constantin

## For Cassidy
—M.R.

## In memory of lovely picnics on the mountain with Nathalie and Patrick
—P.C.

Reading Consultants

### Linda Cornwell
Literacy Specialist

### Katharine A. Kane
Education Consultant
(Retired, San Diego County Office of Education
and San Diego State University)

Library of Congress Cataloging-in-Publication Data
Rockliff, Mara.
  Next to an ant / written by Mara Rockliff ; illustrated by Pascale Constantin.
     p. cm. – (A Rookie reader)
  Summary: A child compares the size of various items and discovers that she is the tallest of all.
  ISBN 0-516-25903-2 (lib. bdg.)  0-516-26830-9 (pbk.)
  [1. Size—Fiction.] I. Constantin, Pascale, ill. II. Title. III.
Series.
PZ7.R5887Ne 2004
[E]—dc22

                                        2003018617

CHILDREN'S PRESS, and A ROOKIE READER®, and associated logos are trademarks and or registered trademarks of Scholastic Library Publishing. SCHOLASTIC and associated logos are trademarks and or registered trademarks of Scholastic Inc.
1 2 3 4 5 6 7 8 9 10 R 13 12 11 10 09 08 07 06 05 04

Next to an ant,
a berry is tall.

Next to a berry,
a snail is tall.

Next to a snail,
a mouse is tall.

Next to a mouse,
my shoe is tall.

9

Next to my shoe,
my cup is tall.

Next to my cup,
my ball is tall.

Next to my ball,
my basket is tall.

Next to my basket,
my puppy is tall.

Next to my puppy,
my brother is tall.

And I?

I am the tallest one of all!

# Word List (25 words)

| | | |
|---|---|---|
| a | brother | puppy |
| all | cup | shoe |
| am | I | snail |
| an | is | tall |
| and | mouse | tallest |
| ant | my | the |
| ball | next | to |
| basket | of | |
| berry | one | |

## About the Author

Next to an ant, Mara Rockliff is very tall indeed. She lives in Charlottesville, Virginia, with her family.

## About the Illustrator

Pascale Constantin was born in Montreal, cultural center of French-speaking Canada. She chose art over hockey at a young age, taking to it like a duck out of water. After many years as a sculptor, Pascale discovered a passion for illustration. Fantastic creatures and funny characters jump from her brushes onto the paper as if by magic. She currently lives in Barbados with her husband, David, and their two very naughty dogs, Lulu and Thor.